SINBAD

Once upon a time, in the faraway city of Bagdad, there lived a young man whose name was Sinbad. He longed for adventure, and that is why he sailed the seven seas.

One day, Sinbad sailed away on one of many journeys. After many days at sea, his ship dropped anchor at a tiny island, and Sinbad and the other sailors stepped ashore to look around.

All at once, the island seemed to grow and rise up out of the water. It was no island, but a monster whale! Suddenly, the whale took a great dive beneath the waves, and everyone fell off into the sea.

All the other sailors managed to swim back to the ship, but poor Sinbad was left behind floating in the water, clinging to a piece of driftwood.

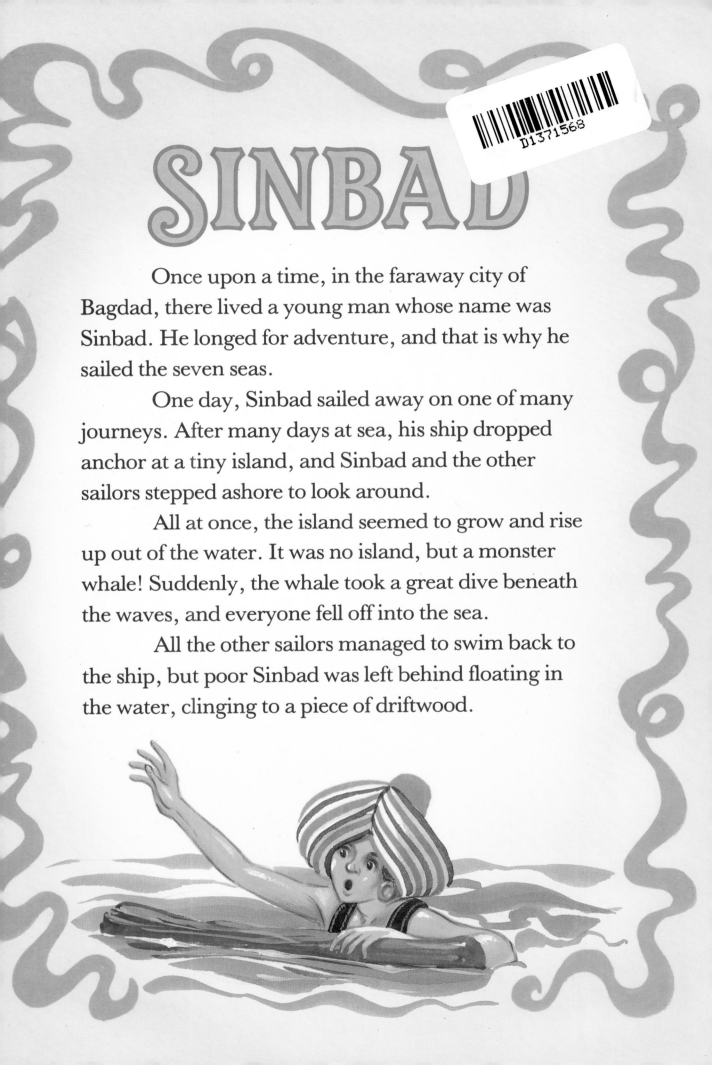

After a while he was washed ashore on another island. He ran across the sandy beach and climbed the tallest palm tree, to try to see his ship. But alas, Sinbad had been left all alone, and his ship was nowhere to be seen.

As he gazed down from the tree, Sinbad noticed a huge white egg on the sand. He slid down the trunk to take a better look. All of a sudden, a big black shadow passed over him. There, circling overhead, was a great white bird — almost as big as the island.

"Now's my chance to escape," thought Sinbad. And when the great white bird flew down onto its egg, Sinbad unwound his turban and tied himself onto the bird's gigantic leg.

Sure enough, the bird flew off carrying Sinbad with him. His plan had worked.

The great bird flew high in the air, through deep valleys and over mountains, until it landed at last, and Sinbad could untie his turban and escape.

The boy found himself in a dry river bed, surrounded by steep cliffs too difficult to climb. He was trapped again.

"How did I get myself into this mess?" Sinbad cried out loudly, and his voice echoed round the cliffs.

All of a sudden, there came a loud hissing noise. All around poor Sinbad large serpents slithered across the floor. Underneath the snakes were huge diamonds and gems — some as big as Sinbad himself.

At the sight of so much treasure, Sinbad's eyes opened wide. Then he remembered the snakes and ran to the nearest cave for safety.

"I can hear voices," cried Sinbad in delight. "Someone is here to rescue me." The boy looked up and saw faces peering over the edge of the cliffs. Men were throwing something onto the rocks below. Could it be huge pieces of meat?

At once, Sinbad understood what was happening. These men threw lumps of meat onto the diamonds near the snakes, then the mountain eagles would swoop down, grab the meat, and carry it back to their nests. Sometimes a few of the diamonds would stick to the meat, and then the men would grab the gems from the eagles' nests.

Sinbad waited for the biggest bird to swoop down. He grabbed the largest diamond he could find and clung onto the bird's legs with all his might.

And that is how our adventurer, Sinbad, escaped the snakes. And that is how he came to be sitting in an eagle's nest with the biggest diamond of them all.

Sinbad returned home a rich man. After a while he got tired of doing nothing and made up his mind to set sail on another voyage.

After many days at sea, his ship dropped anchor in the harbour of a large city.

When the people saw Sinbad and his crew, they begged him for help. ''Our markets are quite empty of fruit. We have nothing to sell and nothing to buy,'' they moaned. ''We have no coconuts or dates, no pomegranates or figs — not even one banana.''

Sinbad looked puzzled, until the people explained, ''Our trees are so tall and smooth, it is impossible for anyone to climb them, except the monkeys.''

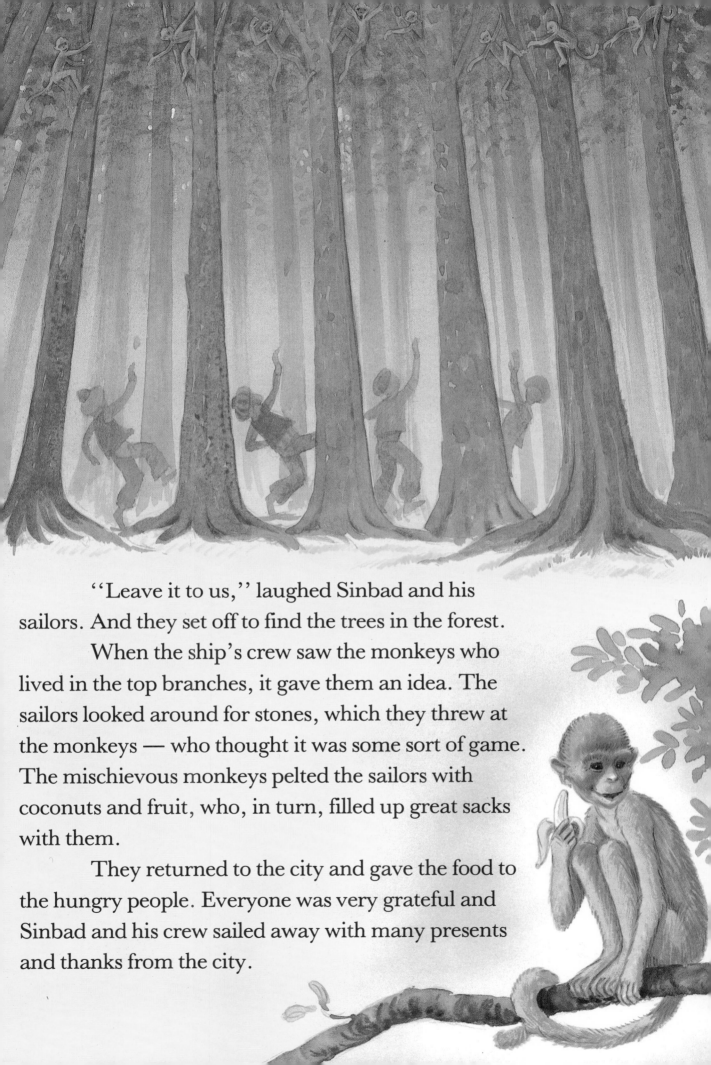

"Leave it to us," laughed Sinbad and his sailors. And they set off to find the trees in the forest.

When the ship's crew saw the monkeys who lived in the top branches, it gave them an idea. The sailors looked around for stones, which they threw at the monkeys — who thought it was some sort of game. The mischievous monkeys pelted the sailors with coconuts and fruit, who, in turn, filled up great sacks with them.

They returned to the city and gave the food to the hungry people. Everyone was very grateful and Sinbad and his crew sailed away with many presents and thanks from the city.

No sooner had Sinbad gone back home to Bagdad, than the Caliph sent for him. ''Set sail at once,'' he commanded, ''and take these gifts to my friend the Sultan of Tasmir Island.''

So once more, Sinbad and his crew put to sea — but alas, on the way, the ship was attacked by pirates, who captured all on board. At the very next port these cruel pirates sold Sinbad and his crew as slaves.

Sinbad was bought by a wealthy merchant who had a lovely daughter. ''Slave,'' grinned the merchant, ''I have a very dangerous task for you,'' and he dragged Sinbad deep into the forest.

"In a few moments the biggest elephant in the world will pass this way to drink at the river. Take this bow and arrow and shoot him," and at that, the merchant pushed Sinbad up the tree and ran away.

All at once, Sinbad could feel the trees shaking. Thundering down the path came an enormous elephant with gleaming tusks. Sinbad shook with fright!

The poor boy trembled so much that he lost his balance and fell out of the tree. He landed on top of the elephant and slid down his trunk onto the ground. Sinbad closed his eyes tight, for he was certain the elephant's great foot would crush him to pulp.

A soft voice was speaking to the great elephant, it was the merchant's daughter. She was standing in the middle of the forest path — feeding him bread and fruit from a silver dish.

Sinbad could hardly believe his eyes. "Don't be afraid," said the girl. "I come here every night to feed this beautiful creature. My father is a cruel man. He wants to kill my elephant and cut off his tusks to sell for ivory."

When the girl put her arms round the beast's great trunk, Sinbad could see how gentle the elephant was.

"Come," smiled Sinbad, "let us escape from here." Quickly he helped the girl onto the elephant. "We will ride away this very night on the elephant's back, and he will carry us back home to Bagdad."

So off they went together travelling over many miles and many lands, until they arrived back safely . . . and lived happily ever after.

THE THREE LITTLE PIGS

Once upon a time, there was a Mother Pig who lived on a farm with her three little piglets, in a warm and comfortable sty.

They were very happy together and got on very well with all the other animals. The farmer gave them plenty to eat. He filled up their trough twice a day with as many turnips and juicy apples as they could manage.

As you may know, pigs are very fond of their food — so it came as no surprise when the little pigs grew too large for the farmyard.

Mother Pig gazed at them with pride, "You have grown so big now, that you must go out into the world and build new houses for yourselves."

As they waved goodbye, their mother gave them some good advice. "Always remember," she said with a tear in her eye, "to beware of the Big Bad Wolf." So, off the three little pigs went, singing and whistling down the road.

Before very long, they came to a stack of straw. "It must be my lucky day," chuckled the first little pig. "I shall build my house with straw, right on this very spot!" Quickly, he gathered up the straw — and in next to no time he had built himself a little house.

The second little pig trotted on until he came to a wood. "How very fortunate I am," giggled the second little pig. "I shall build my house with sticks. This is a good place to live, and I shan't have to carry them far."

So, he set to work and soon had a fine wooden house, with windows and doors and even a wooden chimney. The second little pig felt quite safe from the Big Bad Wolf, so he settled down to eat his dinner.

Now, the third little pig was much wiser than the other two. He planned to build his house of bricks — and had brought along the tools to do the job. He worked very hard for a long time before his house was finished and he was safe inside.

All this time, the Big Bad Wolf had been keeping his eye on the three little pigs.

Sure enough, one dreadful day, the Big Bad Wolf came knocking on the first little pig's door and said, "Little pig, little pig, can I come in?"

"Not by the hair on my chinny chin chin, you cannot come in," squealed the first little pig.

"Then I'll huff and I'll puff and I'll blow your house down," said the wolf. So he huffed and he puffed, and in no time at all the straw house had blown away — and the wolf gobbled up the first little pig.

Next day, the wolf went to see where the second little pig lived. It didn't take him long to find the house made of sticks. When the second little pig heard the wolf coming, he hurried inside and locked the door.

The Big Bad Wolf banged on the door and cried, "Little pig, little pig, can I come in?"

"Not by the hair on my chinny chin chin, you cannot come in," squealed the second little pig.

"Then I'll huff and I'll puff and I'll blow your house down," said the wolf. So he huffed and he puffed, and in no time at all, the stick house just fell to pieces — and the wolf gobbled up the second little pig.

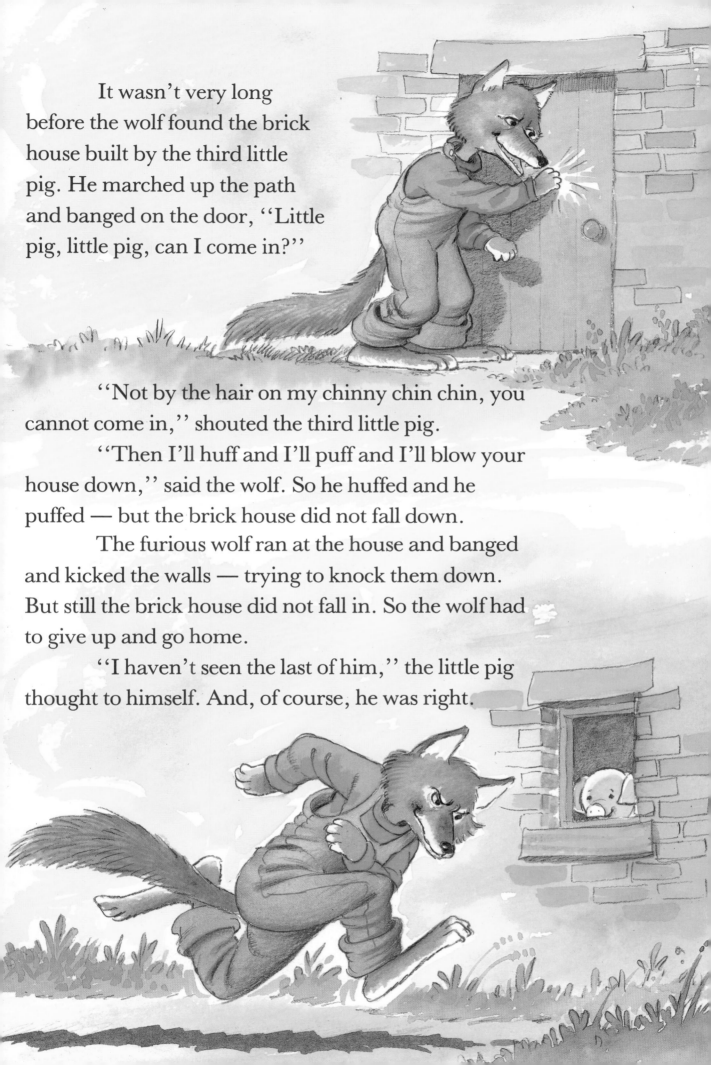

It wasn't very long before the wolf found the brick house built by the third little pig. He marched up the path and banged on the door, "Little pig, little pig, can I come in?"

"Not by the hair on my chinny chin chin, you cannot come in," shouted the third little pig.

"Then I'll huff and I'll puff and I'll blow your house down," said the wolf. So he huffed and he puffed — but the brick house did not fall down.

The furious wolf ran at the house and banged and kicked the walls — trying to knock them down. But still the brick house did not fall in. So the wolf had to give up and go home.

"I haven't seen the last of him," the little pig thought to himself. And, of course, he was right.

That crafty wolf made his mind up to trick the last little pig and make a tasty meal of him. So the very next day the wolf shouted through the little pig's window, "Come with me tomorrow morning at six o'clock and we will dig some turnips for ourselves from the farmer's field."

But, the clever little pig got up an hour early, and when the wolf called for him, he was back safe inside his brick house, eating the turnips.

Then, the wolf said, "Meet me at five tomorrow morning and we can pick apples together from that tree over there."

At four the next morning, the little pig climbed the tree to pick apples. But just as he reached the top, he saw the wolf waiting underneath — ready to eat him.

"These apples are so juicy," called the little pig, throwing one far from the tree. And while the wolf ran after the apple, the clever little pig jumped down and ran all the way home.

Still that Big Bad Wolf wouldn't give up. "Come with me to the fair at four this afternoon," he begged the little pig.

So at two o'clock the third little pig trotted off to the fair to ride on the roundabouts and swings. As he had some money left, he bought himself a butterchurn.

On his way home, as he reached the top of the hill, he spied the wolf coming towards him. So he jumped inside the butterchurn.

It toppled over and began to roll down the hill. Faster and faster it went, until it rolled right over the wolf and knocked him flat. The little pig ran home, shaken, but safe and sound.